This Boxer Books paperback belongs to

. . . .

www.boxerbooks.com

For Elinor, Charlie, and Lee,
who are always good eggs, often silly geese, and sometimes
(in the best possible way) odd ducks

This edition published in Great Britain in 2007
by Boxer Books Limited.
Reprinted twice in 2007.
www.boxerbooks.com

Copyright © 2006 Tad Hills. First published in the
U.S in 2006 by Schwartz & Wade Books, an imprint
of Random House Children's Books. Published by
arrangement with Random House Children's Books,
a division of Random House, Inc. New York, New
York, U.S.A.

Hardback ISBN 10: 1-905417-25-x
Hardback ISBN 13: 978-1-905417-25-4
Paperback ISBN 10: 1-905417-26-8
Paperback ISBN 13: 978-1-905417-26-1

Printed in Italy

Duck & Goose

written & illustrated by Tad Hills

Boxer Books

"Oh my, what is that?" Duck quacked.

"**That's** a silly question," Goose honked.

"It is a big egg, of course."

"Of course it is an egg. I know that!" huffed Duck. "What I mean is, where did it come from?"

Goose looked up to the sky. He looked to the river. He looked to the fields. He thought very hard. "Who are you?" he asked finally.

"I," said Duck, puffing out his feathered chest, "am the one whose egg this is.

I saw it first."

Goose quickly raised one webbed foot. "It's mine.

I touched it first."

"Hey! You should never put your dirty foot on an egg," Duck scolded. "DON'T YOU KNOW ANYTHING ABOUT LOOKING AFTER EGGS?"

"YES, I DO!" Goose cried.

"STOP SHOUTING!" Duck shouted, then whispered forcefully, "Don't *you* know that you and your screaming are likely to disturb the baby bird who is trying to snooze inside this egg?"

Goose wished that Duck wasn't right. He lowered his head and whispered softly, "I'm very sorry. Go back to sleep in there."

"Wow, that's quite a beauty you have," called a blue bird from across the river.

"Thank you, it's mine," quacked Duck.

"Actually, it's mine," honked Goose. "Thank you."

"So," asked Duck, "what do we do now?"

"We should do something," suggested Goose.

Duck thought.

Goose thought.

"Well, we must keep the egg warm until the fuzzy little occupant is ready to come out," said Goose.

"Excellent idea!" exclaimed Duck.

He pushed past Goose.

"Step aside and I shall do just that."

But Goose was quick too.

After a flurry of fussing,

grunting and groaning,

slipping and sliding,

honking and quacking,

Duck and Goose found themselves back to back.

"Budge over, I don't have any room!"
complained Duck.

"You are much closer to me than I am to you."

"Stop yelling in my ear, Goose!"

"Shhhhh," Goose hushed, pointing at the
round thing beneath them.

"Yes, yes, yes, we must remember. Quiet, quiet,
quiet, we mustn't disturb the little one."
And so they sat, very still and very quiet, waiting.

They waited for a long time.

They listened to the crickets chirp and the frogs burp.

"I am going to teach this baby bird to quack like a duck," Duck boasted.

"Well, I am going to teach it to honk like a goose," Goose honked back.

"I'm going to teach this baby bird to waddle," Duck said.

"So am I," Goose added.

They heard the pitter-patter of the rain.

"I'm going to teach this baby bird to swim," Duck said.

"Me too," Goose said.

To pass the time, they sniffed wildflowers in the warm sun and shared breadcrumbs while Goose taught Duck to honk.

They watched the sun set in the sky, and Duck taught Goose to quack.

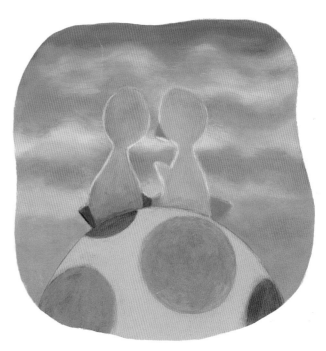

They counted the stars in the night sky.

"Let's teach our baby to fly," said Goose.

"Good idea," said Duck.

"I'm sure our baby will be a fast learner," said Duck.

"If it takes after you and me, I'm sure you're right," agreed Goose.

Together they waited, until—
"Did you feel that, Duck?"
Duck nodded. "Yes! Did you feel that, Goose?"
Goose nodded.
"It's time, Goose, it's time!" Duck squawked.

Quickly, Duck slid down and started
running in circles around their egg.

"What should we do now?"

he shrieked.

"I think we should remain calm,"

Goose cried back.

"Excuse me," a little voice called out.

Duck stopped. In all the exciting confusion, he had failed to notice the blue bird kicking their egg.

"Can I play too?" she asked.

"Play? This is no time for play!" squawked Duck.

"THIS IS NO TIME FOR GAMES!" shouted Goose. "And what's with the kicking?"

"I was only trying to get your attention," said the little bird.

"Well, you got it!" Duck huffed. "False alarm, Goose. Back to work."

"Can't you see that we are very busy here?" Goose explained to the blue bird. "This is serious business. This is perhaps the most important moment of our lives."

"Oh dear, I am sorry," apologised the blue bird. "I had no idea. I just thought that maybe I could play with your ball. It really is a nice one," she added, and then she flew away.

Goose gulped.

"Did she say 'ball'?" he whispered to Duck.

"You know, I did have my doubts," Duck finally said.

"It is a bit squishier than most eggs I've seen."

"Yes, and I must say, I was somewhat suspicious of those big dots," Goose admitted.

"It may not be an egg, but it is lovely," said Duck.

"Oh, absolutely, Duck," Goose agreed. "And it's ours."

As the crickets chirped, the frogs burped, and the grass swayed in a gentle breeze, Goose quacked and Duck honked, and the ball bounced, rolled, and sometimes . . .

even flew.

Other Boxer Books paperbacks

Little Smudge: **Lionel Le Néouanic**

"Hello.
Could I play with you?"
A simple, elegant and innovative tale about the importance of mixing, and making friends and appreciating differences.
ISBN13: 978-1-905417-23-0

Tiger's Story:
Harriet Blackford and Manya Stojic

Tiger's story follows a young tiger cub from playful days with his family to learning how to live alone and take care of himself.
ISBN13: 978-1-905417-42-1

Find Anthony Ant: **Lorna and Graham Philpot**

The ants came marching four by four.
Can you find Anthony Ant?
This delightful counting book is full of clues, deceptive details and an amazing maze!
ISBN13: 978-1-905417-06-3